Disney · PIXAR MOVIE COLLECTION
A SPECIAL DISNEY STORYBOOK SERIES

TOY STORY

PaRragon
Bath · New York · Cologne · Melbourne · Delhi
Hong Kong · Shenzhen · Singapore · Amsterdam

D0248612

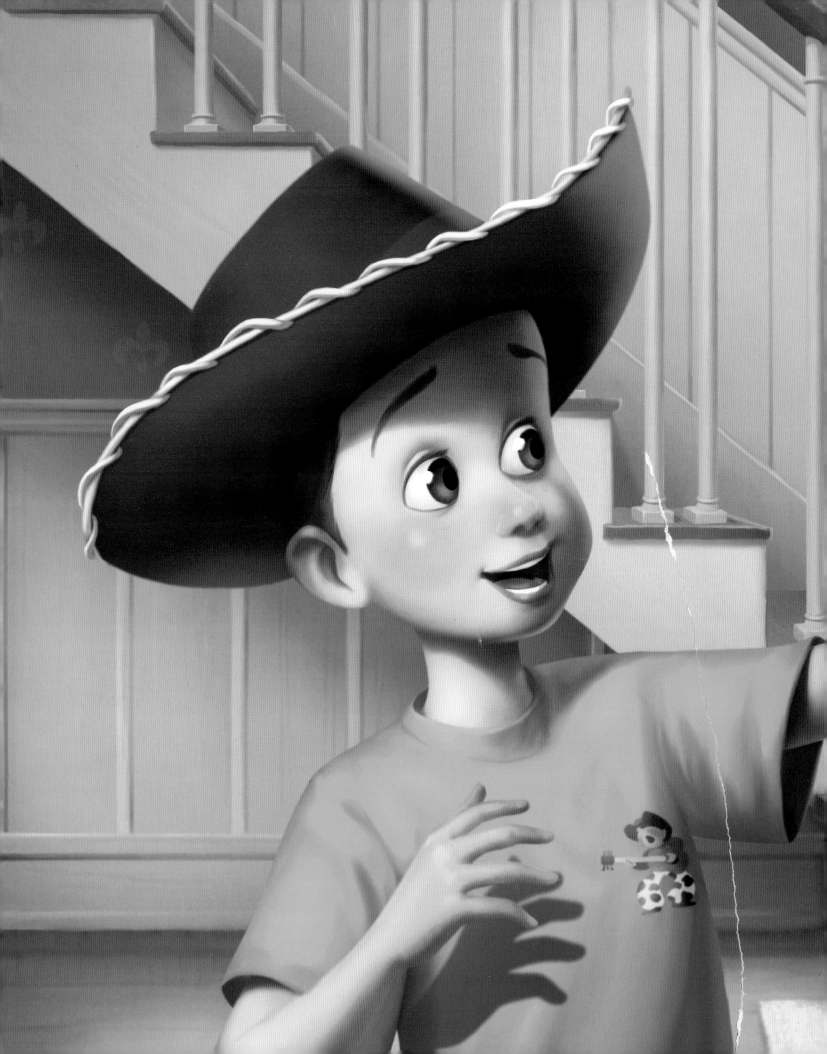

Andy was a young boy with a big imagination. He loved playing with all his toys, but his favourite toy was a cowboy named Woody. "C'mon, Woody!" Andy called, holding the cowboy doll as he ran through the house. Andy took Woody everywhere and the two were the best of friends.

As Andy was playing in his bedroom with Woody, his mum called to him. It was his birthday and it was time for his party.

"See you later, Woody," said Andy as he dropped his friend on his bed and picked up his sister Molly to go downstairs and join his friends. Because he was Andy's favourite toy, Woody even had his own special spot on Andy's bed.

Once Andy had left the room, one by one all the toys started to move. Woody rounded them up from the wardrobe, toy chest and from beneath the bed and everyone chatted – just as they did every time there were no humans around to see them.

Woody had some important news and gathered the toys for a special meeting.

First he reminded everyone that Andy and his family would soon be moving to a new house. Then he blurted out the big news: "Andy's birthday party has been moved to today!"

The toys dreaded Andy's birthday because they were scared that a newer, fancier toy would replace them.

Hamm was peering out through the window when he spotted Andy's guests starting to arrive. "They're here!" he shouted.

The toys watched nervously as Andy's friends arrived with presents.

"They get bigger each year!" Rex cried out anxiously.

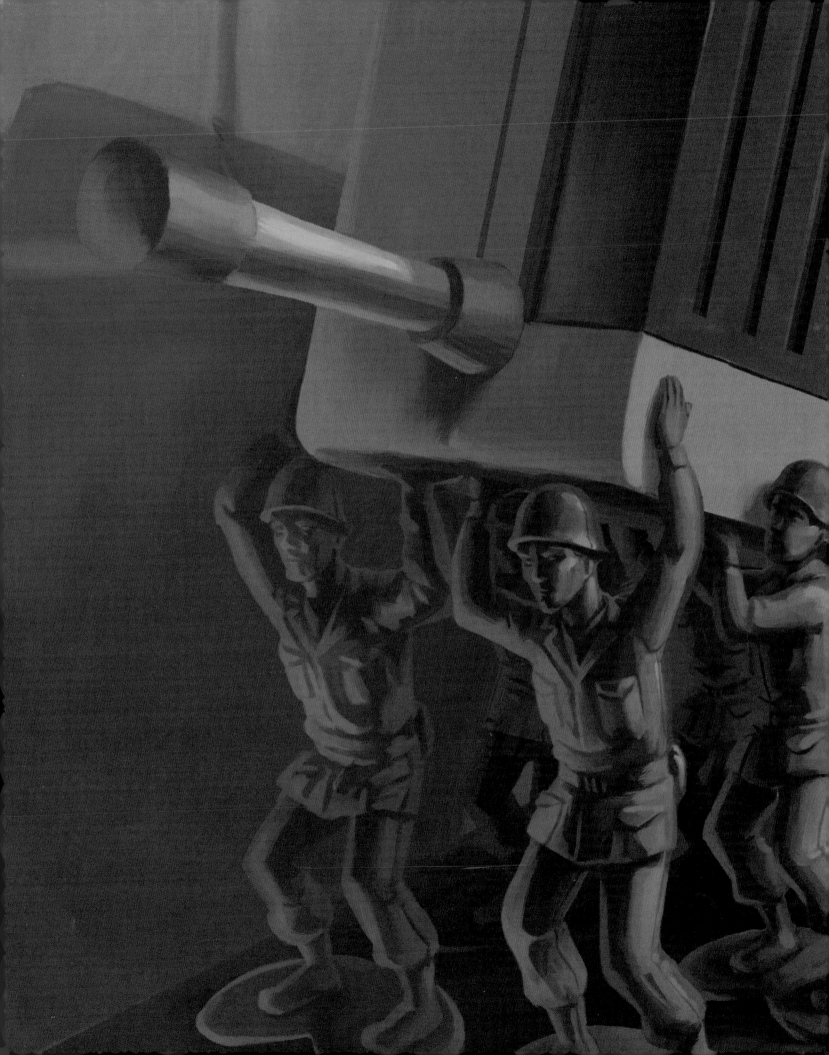

Woody ordered the leader of the Green Army
Men. He wanted them to go downstairs and spy on
Andy's party. "Code red! Sergeant, establish a recon
post downstairs."

They carried a baby monitor out of Andy's room
and sneaked to the top of the stairs. They were
going to use it to listen to Andy and his friends.

The soldiers used a skipping rope to scramble
downstairs so they could set up the baby monitor hidden
behind a plant pot.

The toys upstairs could hear the descriptions of
the presents as they were unwrapped. Luckily, nothing
sounded too threatening ... until the last package.
All the children gasped as they saw....

Just then, the baby monitor cut out! The toys were
frantic as they wanted to know what the last present was.

Suddenly, Andy and his friends burst into the bedroom and then rushed out again, leaving the mystery present on the bed.

"Howdy," Woody said, introducing himself after he climbed on the bed.

The new toy turned and blinked. He stood with his hands on his hips. "I'm Buzz Lightyear, Space Ranger," he declared. He told the toys that he was a space hero who had just landed on Earth.

The new toy also claimed that he could fly and tried to prove it by bouncing off a ball and shouting, "To infinity and beyond!"

The other toys were impressed but Woody just rolled his eyes. "That's just falling with style," he claimed.

Nothing was the same after Buzz arrived.
Cowboy posters on the wall were replaced
with space posters. Andy stopped wearing his
cowboy hat and ran through the house dressed
in a space costume instead.

Buzz was also popular with
the other toys – everyone
wanted to spend time with him.

But the thing that upset Woody the most was seeing Andy climb under his new Buzz Lightyear cover with Buzz. Woody was left in the toy chest, alone and forgotten. He was no longer Andy's favourite toy.

One evening, Andy's mum suggested that they go to Andy's favourite restaurant, Pizza Planet. Andy could only take one toy with him and Woody wanted to make sure he was chosen.

When Buzz got knocked out of the bedroom window by accident the other toys thought Woody had done it on purpose.

"You didn't want to face the fact that Buzz might be Andy's favourite toy, so you got rid of him!" Mr Potato Head accused Woody.

Just then, Andy ran into the room and searched
high and low for Buzz. When he couldn't find him,
he picked up Woody instead and left for Pizza Planet.
As Andy, his sister and mum got ready to set off,
a small figure emerged from the bushes and leaped
on to the back of the car. It was Buzz!

When Andy's mum stopped at a petrol station, Buzz jumped on to the back seat of the car next to Woody.

"Buzz! You're alive!" Woody exclaimed in relief.

But Buzz wasn't pleased to see Woody.

"Even though you tried to terminate me, revenge is not an idea we promote on my planet," Buzz said. Then his eyes narrowed. "But we're not on my planet, are we?" Buzz jumped on to Woody, and the two began to fight! As they wrestled angrily, they tumbled out of the car and on to the pavement.

Suddenly, Andy's mum drove off – without them! Woody and Buzz were stranded.

Luckily, Woody spotted a Pizza Planet delivery lorry. The lorry could take him to Andy! But Woody knew he couldn't face the other toys without Buzz. So he tricked Buzz, saying that the lorry was a space shuttle that could return him to his home planet.

At Pizza Planet, Woody quickly spotted Andy. With a little luck, he figured, they could jump into Molly's pushchair.

"Okay, Buzz, get ready and ... Buzz?" Woody turned round to see the space ranger running towards the Rocket Ship Crane Game. Buzz thought it was a real spaceship.

Buzz climbed into the Rocket Ship Crane Game. Woody followed, still hoping he could convince Buzz to return home.

Suddenly, the machine started whirring. Then the claw dropped – and grabbed onto Buzz. Woody grabbed Buzz's feet and tried to drag him back down, but it was no use. Both toys were pulled into the air and dropped into the prize slot.

"Yes! Double prizes!" shouted the kid, seeing the two toys.

To Woody's horror, he saw that the boy was Sid, Andy's nasty neighbour.

All the toys in Andy's room knew Sid. He lived next door and was the meanest kid on the street. Many times, Andy's toys had looked out of the window and seen Sid torturing toys in his back garden. Sometimes he even blew them up – just for fun!

Now Sid looked at Buzz and Woody with glee. "Let's go home and ... play!" he said with a wicked laugh. Woody knew they were doomed.

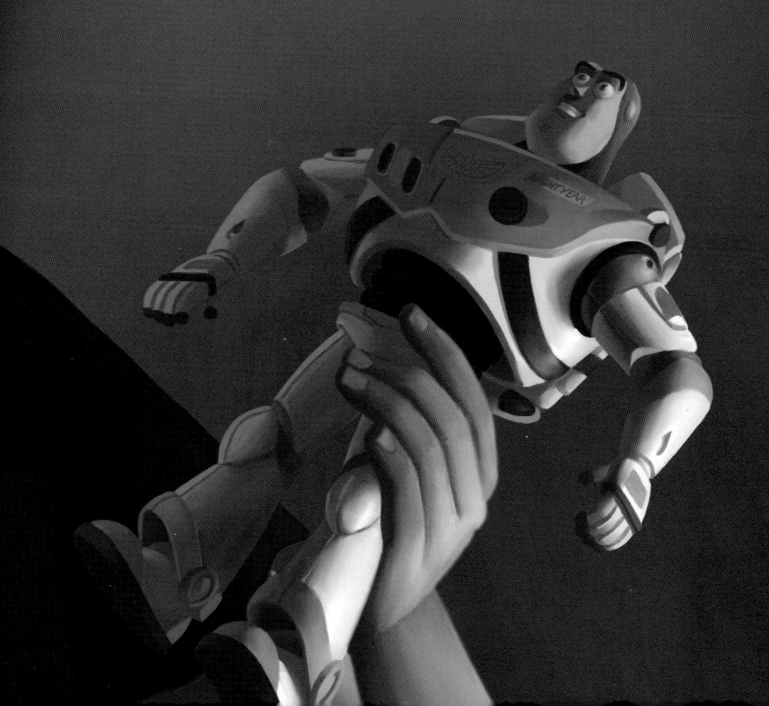

Sid took Woody and Buzz home and left them in his bedroom. The room was dark and eerie and Sid had lots of scary tools that he used for toy 'operations'.

As Woody and Buzz looked around nervously they heard strange rustling sounds – distorted toys were creeping out of the darkness. Sid had modified his toys and turned them into terrifying 'mutants'.

Trying to escape, Buzz and Woody ran into the hall – and straight into Scud, Sid's vicious dog! Panicked, the two toys fled.

A FLYING TOY

Buzz ducked through an open door. Inside, he suddenly heard,
"Calling Buzz Lightyear! This is Star Command!" Then the voice
continued: "The world's greatest superhero, now the world's greatest toy!"
It was a TV commercial for Buzz Lightyear toys!
Buzz's mouth fell open in shock.

Buzz felt stunned. Was the TV ad true? Still in shock, he walked to the stairs and saw blue sky through the hall window. He knew he could fly ... couldn't he? Wasn't he a space ranger? Gathering courage, he climbed to the top of the stair railing – and leaped. "To infinity and beyond!" he cried.

For a moment, Buzz seemed to hang in the air. Then, gravity took over. Buzz fell – CRASH! – on to the stair landing, and his left arm broke off.

Buzz Lightyear finally and completely understood the truth: he was a toy.

Upstairs, Woody searched for Buzz. He peeked into a bedroom and saw Sid's little sister, Hannah, playing with her dolls.

After Buzz fell down the stairs, Hannah had found the space ranger and added him to her tea party. She didn't mind that his arm was broken. Most of her toys were broken already, thanks to Sid's 'operations'.

Woody waited until Hannah left the room, then ran to help Buzz. But Buzz didn't want to cooperate. He was upset because he wasn't a real space ranger. "Look at me," he moaned. "I can't even fly out of the window."

The window! That gave Woody an idea!

Woody ran to Sid's bedroom window
and waved towards Andy's house.
"Hey, guys!"

Looking outside from their own window, Andy's
toys were surprised to see Woody. The cowboy threw
them a string of Christmas lights – an escape line from
Sid's bedroom.

But the toys still didn't trust Woody. And Buzz refused
to come to the window to prove he was all right. Using
Buzz's broken arm, Woody tried to pretend everything
was fine – but that made it look like he'd hurt Buzz!

Disappointed, Andy's toys dropped the lights and
walked away.

Woody felt terrible. And when he turned back into
Sid's room, things seemed to be getting even worse –
the mutant toys had surrounded Buzz!

Woody tried to fight them off but they grabbed Buzz's arm and pushed Woody away. Then, after a moment, the mutants stepped away from the space ranger. Buzz sat up in surprise, flexing his left arm, which was now attached and working perfectly. Sid's mutant toys had fixed him!

Even though they looked scary, the mutant toys were friendly.

Suddenly, the toys heard Sid racing up the stairs. Everyone scattered – except for Buzz, who wouldn't move. He was still sad because he wasn't a real space ranger.

When Sid burst into the room, he strapped a rocket on to Buzz's back. Blast-off was scheduled for the next morning.

Trapped under a crate, Woody pleaded with Buzz to escape and return to Andy. "Over in that house is a kid who thinks you are the greatest. And it's not because you're a space ranger. It's because you're a toy. You are *his* toy," Woody said. "You are a cool toy!"

Woody nearly lost hope, but Buzz finally realized Woody was right. Being a toy was important.

The space ranger knew it was time to get back to Andy! He ran over to Woody – to help the cowboy break free, too.

Just then, the alarm clock started ringing. Sid jumped out of bed. "Time for lift-off!" he yelled, grabbing Buzz and running outside.

Woody knew he had to do something fast. As soon as Sid left, Woody gathered the mutant toys together and laid out a rescue plan. Buzz was a good toy, he explained, and they couldn't let him get blown up. "We'll have to break a few rules," he told the mutants. "But if it works, it'll help everyone."

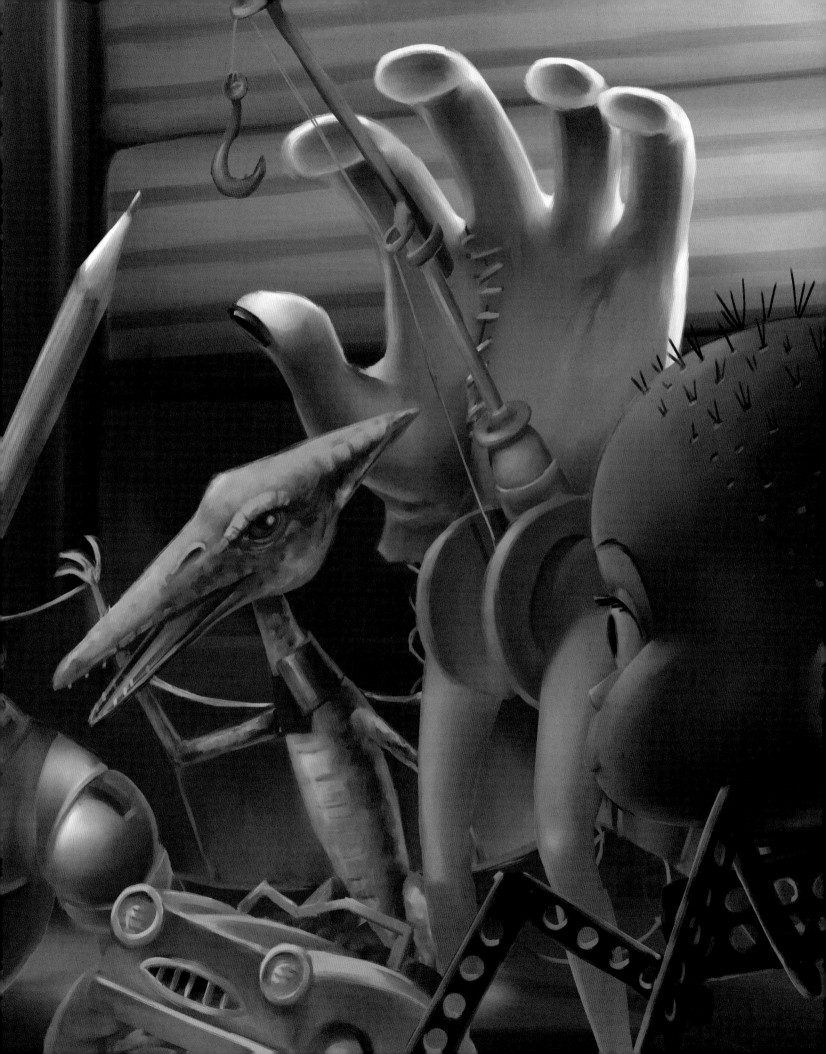

Some of the mutants distracted Scud and Hannah, while Woody and the others jumped on to a skateboard and raced down the stairs, shooting out into the back garden.

Outside, Sid prepared to launch Buzz into outer space. With a cruel grin, he leaned over to light the big rocket's fuse as he began the countdown. "Ten, nine, eight, seven...."

Suddenly, he heard –

"Reach for the sky!" It was Woody, lying nearby.

Sid turned and stared. He picked Woody up. How had the cowboy doll got outside? Was something wrong with its pull string? Then, one by one, the mutant toys stood up and staggered out of the sandbox ... splashed out of the mud puddle ... and crawled from under the dog dish! Together, slowly and steadily, they surrounded the shocked boy.

But Woody wasn't done with Sid. "From now on, you must take good care of your toys. Because if you don't, we'll find out," Woody warned. And then he leaned in very close and looked Sid right in the eye. "So play nice!"

"AAAHH!" Sid threw up his arms and shrieked in terror. Screaming, he ran into the house and slammed the door.

The toys cheered – their plan had worked! Buzz was saved! And best of all, Sid's days of torturing toys were over.

But Woody and Buzz couldn't stand around and cheer – a moving van was in front of Andy's house! It was the day of the big move and if they didn't hurry, Andy would leave without them.

Quickly, the two toys ran towards Andy's house. But Buzz couldn't fit through the fence because the rocket was still attached to his back.

"Just go, I'll catch up," Buzz assured Woody.

But Woody wouldn't leave without his friend. By the time Woody helped Buzz through the fence, though, it was too late. Andy's car had driven off.

Woody and Buzz dashed after the moving van, determined to catch up.
Buzz grabbed a loose strap, then climbed up on to the rear of the van.
He tried to help Woody up, too.

"Come on! You can do it, Woody!" Buzz shouted.

But Scud had seen the two toys and he raced right after them. The dog
leaped up and grabbed Woody in his mouth, dragging him off the van.

"Nooooo!" Buzz yelled. He jumped on to Scud's head to save Woody.

Now Woody was safe, but Buzz was left behind, trapped by Scud.

Woody yanked open the back of the van and looked through the boxes until he found RC Car. Using the remote control, Woody sent RC back to pick up Buzz.

But Andy's toys didn't understand what Woody was doing, and angrily threw him off!

Luckily, Buzz and RC picked up Woody as they came speeding back. Finally realizing what had really happened, the other toys tried to help ...

... but RC's batteries ran out. Woody watched, heartbroken, as the van moved further and further away.

Then they realized – Buzz still had the rocket on his back! Once the fuse was lit, Woody whooped with excitement.

"You did it!" Buzz cried. "Next stop: Andy!"

As the rocket began to burn, RC picked up speed, zooming down the street faster and faster. Buzz and Woody hung on tight as the van came back into view. But by now, the little car was whizzing so fast, they began to lift off the ground!

As they rose upward, Woody let go of RC, who landed in the van. Buzz and Woody whooshed into the sky.

Just as the rocket was about to explode, Buzz snapped open his space wings and broke free.

"Buzz, you're flying!" Woody exclaimed.

"This isn't flying," Buzz replied.
"This is falling with style!"

Buzz and Woody soared through the sky, then glided down towards Andy's car. While Andy was looking out of the window, the two dropped unnoticed through the car's open sunroof, landing safely on the back seat.

Hearing a thump, Andy looked over. "Woody! Buzz!" he shouted. He hugged them close, thrilled to have his two favourite toys back.

Woody and Buzz had made it home.

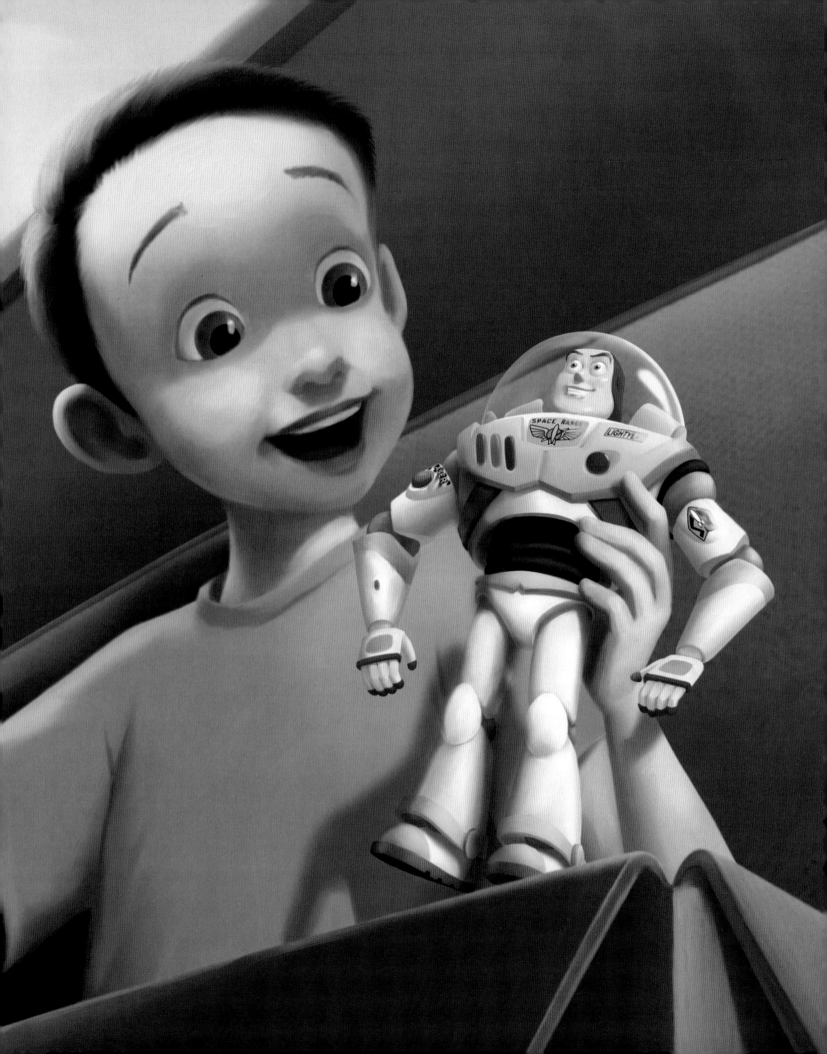

Everyone settled happily into the new house.
But all too soon, it was Christmas – which meant new toys.

"You aren't worried, are you?" Woody asked Buzz, as they sat listening to the baby monitor.

"No, no," Buzz replied nervously. "Are you?"

"Now, Buzz, what could Andy possibly get that is worse than you?" Woody teased.

They listened intently as Andy unwrapped his first present … and suddenly Buzz and Woody's eyes widened, as they heard an unmistakable sound: woof-woof!